MW00427323

inked HOLIDAY

A MEN OF INKED SHORT STORY

www.chellebliss.com

CHELLE BLISS

USA TODAY BESTSELLING AUTHOR

A MESSAGE FROM CHELLE BLISS

Dear Reader,

I hope you love this short visit with the Gallos. I hope it gives you all the feels, warms you on a cold night, and puts a goofy smile on your face.

I hinted to this short story in Cinder, Men of Inked Heatwave #13 and I've heard your pleas for me write this little feel-good story. It wasn't as easy as I thought it would be. Heck, at one point, I deleted half the book by accident and was never able to recover it.

The Gallos aren't over. There's so much more to come.

Thank you for wanting more of my family and allowing me to live in a wonderful dream.

Inked Holiday Copyright 2023

This is a work of fiction. Names, characters, places, and incidents either are the product of the author's imagination or are used fictitiously, and any resemblance to actual persons, living or dead, business establishments, events, or locales is entirely coincidental. The publisher does not assume any responsibility for third-party websites or their content.

All Rights Reserved. No part of this book may be reproduced, scanned, or distributed in any printed or electronic format without permission.

❄

Publisher © Bliss Ink December 20th 2023
Edited by Lisa A. Hollett
Proofread by Shelley Charlton
Cover Design © Chelle Bliss

gigi

. . .

I STEP out of the SUV, the soles of my shoes crunching against the snow. A shiver instantly runs through me from the foreign sensation. "I'm not a cold-weather girl, but the clothes are top-notch," I say to Pike as he climbs out of the vehicle, looking ridiculously handsome in his jacket and hat. The tight jeans hugging his ass don't hurt either.

"You look sexy as hell. Good enough to eat, darlin'." He gives me a wink before he opens the back door for Harley and pokes his head inside. "Come on, baby," he says to our daughter, always patient and sweet with her. "We're here."

"Finally," she grumbles, grouchy after falling asleep on the long ride.

Harley places her hand in Pike's and jumps out of

the SUV, taking off into the snow. She bends down, scooping up a handful before throwing it in the air. "It's like magic," she whispers, staring up as the flakes fly back toward her face. She closes her eyes and smiles with nothing but pure joy.

I tip my head toward their big black truck that stands out against the white background of the snowy mountains. "Well, Tamara and Mammoth beat us here."

"No one's going to outdrive Mammoth. The guy loves speed," Pike says like I don't already know this.

There's nothing more terrifying than climbing into his back seat. My cousin Tamara isn't any better either. The girl has always loved living on the edge, and her husband Mammoth feeds into that with his fast engines and the stupid amount of horsepower that all of his vehicles have.

I take a step and freeze, but not from the cold. "Ugh," I groan, trying to shake off the way the skin on the back of my neck crawls with every movement.

"You'll get used to it," he says, knowing exactly why I'm about to have a meltdown.

But I don't care if we lived here for a decade—I would never get used to the feeling. I thought I couldn't hate anything more than sand between my toes, but this has it beat by a mile.

"Hey, watch me," Harley says as she raises her arms and falls backward with a thud. Her arms stay extended as she moves them up and down. "Mom, you see it?"

I giggle at her silliness, but a warmth comes over me at the happiness on her face. "You're making a great snow angel, baby. Good job."

She's made them before, but only in the sand. It isn't the same, and she's always dreamed of being able to do it in the snow one day. It is nice to see her little-girl dreams coming true.

"Yes!" she squeals, moving her arms faster. If she does it for much longer, she'll hit the grass that's hidden beneath the snow.

"This feels like Christmas," I say, sucking in a deep breath through my nose. The smells are different from back home. There's no salt in the air. No damp humidity that's tinged with mold similar to an old shoe. Instead, there's a fresh crispness to the air.

"It feels like my childhood," Pike admits, his face unreadable, but I have no doubt there're a million emotions brewing underneath his stoic façade.

I ignore the crunch under my feet and move toward him. "Are you okay?" I ask as I wrap my arms around him, trying to feel his body underneath all the layers of clothing we're both wearing.

He peers down at me with a small, sad smile. "I am. I've come to terms with what my childhood was like. There were some good memories. Most of them around the holidays, so this isn't a bad thing for me, darlin'." He bends his neck, brushing his cold lips against my forehead. "It's stirring up mostly happy things."

I press my cheek to his chilly jacket. "Christmas should always be happy. Maybe my grandpa was onto something this year. I'm glad we got away to somewhere snowy."

Pike chuckles as he hugs me. "That's only because we get to go back to warm weather."

As we're standing there, Lily and Jett's white truck pulls through the entrance to the sprawling property. They had been following us but had to pull off for a potty break for Celeste.

"This place is really something," Pike says as they come to a stop behind our SUV.

"Mom found it online."

The property is deep in the mountains of North Carolina. There're over a dozen cabins, but they aren't small and quaint. Each one has multiple bedrooms, big enough for us to split off by generation.

Our family has filled two of the cabins on the property with our size, which continues to grow year after year. There's a main lodge with some amenities, even though every cabin is stocked with a full kitchen and everything someone could want in their usual home.

"Want to curl up by the fire tonight?" Pike asks.

"You think Lily, Jett, Mammoth, and Tamara are going to let us have the fireplace alone?" I ask into the fabric of his jacket, trying to protect my face from the wind.

"Nope," he clips out. "Doesn't matter. Each bedroom has its own fireplace. I think I'm getting lucky on that bearskin rug I saw that's in front of each one too."

"Only if you're a good boy."

He peers down at me again, but this time with a smirk. "Darlin', I'm always a good boy except when you want me to be naughty."

"Hey. Hey. Sorry about being late," Lily says as she hops down from Jett's truck. "Celeste overdid it on the juice boxes in the car and couldn't hold it any longer."

"It's cool. No worries," I tell her, but then I see the same look on her face that I had when I first stepped out of the SUV. "Snow sucks."

It makes me feel good that I'm not the only one who's grossed out by the feeling.

She lifts one leg and then the other, looking as if

she's about to throw up. "Oh. My. God. I don't know if I can deal with this all week."

"Maybe we'll get used to it," I say, trying to give her hope, but I'm sure she knows there is none...just like I do.

"It's worse than sand, and I freaking hate sand." She pretends to heave. "Baby, carry me," she says to Jett as he steps out of the truck, carrying her purse and probably five-hour-old coffee. "I can't do this."

Jett just shakes his head, laughing. "Who's going to carry all this, then?"

"Leave it in the snow. My body and mental health are far more important."

Jett lifts the strap of her purse over his head, securing it around his body. "Celeste, can you carry Mom's coffee?" he asks his daughter, not realizing she's already heading toward Harley.

I love Jett. He's the perfect husband for Lily. I've known Jett my entire life, and never in my wildest dreams did I think they'd ever become a couple, let alone get married. But somehow, they work. He dotes on her, treating her like an absolute princess.

"Snow angels," Celeste calls out, not hearing her father as she falls backward next to Harley, screeching with excitement.

"Leave the coffee," Lily tells him again, wiggling

her fingers at him like she's in distress. "It's old and cold like me." Lily snorts, her nose turning a dark shade of pink from the freezing air.

The front door to the cabin swings open, and Tamara steps outside, holding her sweater closed and her shoulders high. "What in the hell are you guys doing? Get in here before you die from hypothermia." She leans against the wood pillar on the porch, looking like she belongs here.

"Coming," Lily calls out before Jett scoops her up in his arms.

"You will soon enough, mama," he says to her, and it takes everything in me not to throw up a little in my mouth.

She drops her head back, laughing. "You're not the sweet-talker you think you are," she says to him, one arm wrapped around his neck with her body plastered tightly against him.

"Want me to carry you too?" Pike asks as Jett carries her toward the cabin.

I pull out of his warm embrace. "No. I need to get used to the feeling, or else I'm going to be miserable all week. I need to go outside sometime eventually."

"I plan to keep you plenty busy inside, darlin'."

I slap his chest with the back of my hand. "This isn't our honeymoon. This is a *family* vacation."

"They get your days, and I get your nights."

I motion toward the front porch, where Lily, Jett, and Tamara are watching us like we're moving at a snail's pace. "I'm sure they'll have something to say about that."

"I'm pretty sure we won't be the only ones, and if they have a problem with me wanting to enjoy my wife, they'll have to find other ways to keep themselves entertained."

God, I love my husband.

lily

...

"HOLY MOLY," I whisper as I spin around, trying to wrap my head around the massive size and indescribable beauty of the cabin.

Even though I'd seen pictures online, I thought they were a camera trick. I expected the place to be much smaller than it is. There's wood everywhere, and the fireplace in the main room is enormous and crackling with flames.

"It's something, isn't it?" Tamara says, looking around the place. "Wait until you see the other rooms."

I bend down, placing my hand on the wall to keep my balance. The multiple layers, heavy coat, and winter boots have me completely out of sorts. I haven't felt this way since I was pregnant. "I don't think I could get used to wearing this many layers all the time."

Gigi comes to my side and works the laces on her boots. "Next time, I'm getting slip-ons. Lace-up boots are the stupidest shit ever. I don't know why I thought it was a good idea."

I snort as I yank at my laces, which I tied way too tight, making them almost impossible to undo. "I much prefer my flip-flops and tank tops."

"That ain't no lie," Tamara says as she leans back on the leather couch.

"Yo," Mammoth says as he trots down the steep wooden steps like he'd been doing his whole life. "The bedrooms are insane. There's a fireplace in each one."

"It's settled. I'm never getting out of bed," Tamara says as she tucks her legs underneath her body while she curls up.

"I like the sound of that," Mammoth mutters.

There's a knock on the front door before it opens.

"Oh good. You're all here," Aunt Suzy says as she walks into the cabin, looking more like a snowman than a human. She's covered in a coating of snow and wearing an oversized, puffy white coat that almost touches her ankles. "I'm glad you guys made it. They're calling for a blizzard tonight."

"What?" I ask, slightly panicked. I've never experienced a blizzard and have no idea what to expect. "What's that mean? Are we going to be okay?"

Aunt Suzy waves her hand out in front of herself. "It just means we're going to get a lot of snow and shouldn't drive anywhere, but we weren't planning on leaving the property anyway. Don't worry, sweetie."

I'm still struggling with my coat, unable to get it off my body and about ready to scream. Jett's somehow removed his coat and winter gear like he'd done it a thousand times before.

When he tosses his coat onto a nearby chair, he moves his gaze to me, noticing my trouble. "Let me help you," he says, carefully peeling it off me.

"Thank you," I say to him as the last part of it slides over my wrist. "I was feeling claustrophobic."

"We're going to the lodge tonight for an early dinner. We're hoping everyone will join us," Suzy says, adjusting the furry hat on her head. "We have reservations at five."

"Can the restaurant handle all of us, Ma?" Gigi asks as she tosses her jacket on a nearby chair.

"They can, but let me know ahead of time if you guys don't want to go. We're spreading the word, going cabin to cabin."

"You could've texted us instead of trudging through the cold and snow," Gigi tells her mother as she shakes out her hair.

Suzy shakes her head as she stares at her daughter. "What fun would that have been?"

"It would've been a hell of a lot warmer."

"I like the cold. It's the perfect excuse to snuggle with your father." Suzy grins.

"Ma." Gigi lifts up her hands, not wanting to hear more. "Stop."

"That's sweet, Aunt Suzy," I tell her, snuggling under Jett's arm as I still try to warm my bones.

I love how Aunt Suzy and Uncle Joe love each other. Over all the years, their affection for and devotion to each other hasn't waned even a little bit.

"Well, I'm going to run. It's a long walk back to my cabin, or at least it feels like it is in this weather."

"Bye, Ma," Gigi calls out.

"Want an escort?" Pike asks, always being a gentleman...at least with his mother-in-law.

"No, baby. You stay here and stay warm. Joe's outside, talking to the girls as they make snow angels." She turns back around and reaches for the door handle. "Let me know by four if you're coming."

Jett chuckles softly, and I smack his back. "Behave," I whisper.

"Got it, Auntie," Tamara says before Suzy disappears into the cold.

"Where are the kids sleeping?" Gigi asks Tamara.

"Top floor. It's a kid's paradise up there. All bunk beds, couches, a giant television, and other shit."

"We won't see them much all week, then?" Gigi asks.

"Nope," Tamara replies, shaking her head. "I bet they'll take turns going to the other cabin to see what they have too."

"I would've loved this when we were young."

"There's no rule that says we can't go up there and play now," Pike says to her as he sits down on the armrest of the couch next to her.

"You want to get unpacked?" Jett asks me.

I tip my head back, staring up at my husband. "Are you trying to get me alone?"

The smirk on his face tells me everything I need to know. "If I have my way, we're taking home a lifelong souvenir."

"Jett," I whisper, peering around the room, but no one's paying any attention to us. "Are you sure? Celeste is basically self-sufficient. Do you really want to start all over again? Diapers, feedings, and lack of sleep. I'm not sure we can do it all at our age."

"One hundred percent, but only if you want to. This time will be easier."

That's easy for him to say. He won't have to push a human being out of his body and waddle around for months before that, dealing with heartburn, stretch marks, and sore breasts.

But the thought of a little one in my arms again gives me all the warm fuzzies. I feel like Celeste's younger years went by in the blink of an eye. I was too worried about anything going wrong that I'm not sure I allowed myself to fully enjoy all the little moments.

I turn back to face him, and my stomach fills with butterflies. "I do. I want another little one."

The heat of his hands warms me as he rubs my arms. "More than one?" he asks with an eyebrow raised.

"One at a time, Jett. Who knows if I can even get pregnant again."

"Lil, if I have my way, we're going to have twins."

I laugh at the absurdity as I place my hand on his chest. "Good thing for me, you can't wish that into existence."

"What about twins?" Gigi asks, listening in on our private conversation.

"Lily's going to have twins," Jett announces.

Tamara gasps and uncurls her body. Gigi looks stunned, not even able to form words as her mouth hangs open.

"When?" Mammoth asks.

"I'm not pregnant," I tell everyone. "Relax."

"I'm wishing them into existence," Jett informs them.

Gigi rolls her eyes as Tamara waves off his stupidity.

"You about gave me a heart attack," Tamara says, letting her body go boneless again. "There's nothing about twins that even remotely sounds fun. Double the babies, double the diapers."

"I could do it," Jett says.

I roll my eyes this time. "He says that now, until it's four in the morning, and there're two babies covered in shit and screaming to be fed."

"It's my Christmas wish," Jett says, pulling me back into an embrace.

"Did you ask Santa for them?" Mammoth mocks him, grabbing a beer out of the beverage fridge in the bar area of the great room.

"I did, and I've been a very, very good boy this year."

Mammoth grunts. "I've been one too, but I'd rather eat my own foot than have twins."

"Baby," Tamara snaps, "Don't say that. You're going to put the bad mojo out there, and I'm going to end up knocked up with triplets with how my luck is sometimes."

I laugh at the absurdity of this entire conversation.

I'm older now, and so are my eggs. Most likely, I can't even get pregnant without a ton of effort.

"Twins and triplets don't just happen," I tell them.

Gigi shakes her head as she grips her forehead. "Listen, there weren't any twins in my mom's family, and *boom*...Luna and Rosie. So, don't think it's impossible. I've realized nothing in this world is impossible anymore."

The door to the cabin opens again, and Celeste and Harley come in giggling.

"I'm a popsicle." Celeste shivers, rubbing her arms through her heavy coat.

"You two were in the snow and cold a long time. Take off your boots and coats and come warm up in front of the fire," Gigi tells them, motioning for them to join her and Tamara in front of the fireplace.

"Want to see our room?" Jett asks me, his eyes filled with so much sin.

"Yes," I whisper to him. "But no trying yet. Not until later."

"Baby, I just want to unpack. Everyone's awake, and with what I have planned for you tonight, I don't want any witnesses."

My eyes widen at his words and the promise of a very hot night.

tamara

. . .

"WE CAN STAY in and play Trivial Pursuit," Lily says as she leans back against Jett as they sit on the floor in front of the fireplace.

I turn my gaze toward Gigi, giving her a look. There isn't a person in this room who could beat Lily in a game of trivia. The girl spent most of her life with her nose buried in a book. A fun evening on vacation, blizzard or not, would never include losing at a game that's geared toward the smart people.

"Babe," Gigi says, uncurling her body from the couch, "I'm going to be wiped after dinner. I don't think I'll have the brain capacity to play a hardcore game of trivia. I'm thinking something a little less brain-heavy."

"Strip poker," Mammoth says as he stands behind the couch with his hands on my shoulders.

All eyes in the room turn to him, including mine.

"Have you lost your mind?" I ask him.

He shakes his head. "It's easy and fun."

I raise an eyebrow at my husband. "Fun for whom?"

"Regular poker, then," he replies.

"I'm game for poker, but not strip poker," Jett says, "I'm not sharing my wife's body with anyone."

Mammoth leans over, bringing his mouth next to my ear. "It was a shock to the system. No one's thinking about Trivial Pursuit now, princess. The only woman I want to see naked is you."

I pull back, keeping my narrowed eyes on him. "You better not want to see them."

He smirks at me, the same way he has since the day we met. It always makes my toes curl. "It was a trick, and it worked."

"We could sing Christmas carols," Lily says.

Sometimes I swear Lily and I can't be related. We have almost nothing in common, but I still love her to bits, even if she's a little more on the nerdy side. Hell, she's a lot more.

"That's a giant no," Gigi says, shaking her head. "Never happening. I'd rather spend the night on my hands and knees, scrubbing all these wood floors, than singing Christmas songs."

"Spending the night on your hands and knees doesn't sound half bad." Pike winks at his wife and is immediately met with a middle finger from Gigi.

"I say we let the parents handle the kids, and we head over to the lodge bar and partake in some refreshments," I tell them. "I could use one or three after that road trip."

"Just us or everyone?" Lily asks.

"Everyone," I say. "The entire gang."

"A night without the kids?" Gigi pulls on her lower lip, and I can see the debate in her eyes. "I'm not sure the kids will be happy about that."

"Dude," I say, drawing out the word. "They'll be happy to have a night with our parents. They give the kids all the sugar they want."

"Harley," Gigi calls out, looking toward the stairs.

A few seconds later, I hear clomping on the stairs, but it's more than just Harley coming downstairs.

"Yeah?" Harley asks, dressed like she's at a high-class ski resort instead of in the middle of nowhere. "Is something wrong?"

"Do you want to spend the night with Grandma and Grandpa?"

Harley's eyes light up. "Uh, yeah, Mom. Why wouldn't I?"

I chuckle to myself, having known that was going to be the answer. What kid wouldn't want to spend the night with their grandparents? Especially the ones in our family.

Gigi sighs. "Okay. We're going to go out tonight, but I wanted to make sure you guys would be okay without us."

Not only Harley, but Jackson, Riley, and Celeste all do a happy-dance celebration. If I weren't so excited about a grown-up night at the bar with my cousins, my feelings would be slightly hurt.

"Guess that answers that," Mammoth mutters behind me. "We won't be missed."

Lily opens her arms, and Celeste runs to her and falls into her lap. "Will you be okay without us?" she asks her daughter, as if she didn't just witness something close to a touchdown celebration at the Super Bowl.

"Yes, Momma. I love spending time with Grandma and Grandpa, especially when Grandpa lets us make him into a mummy and he chases us around the house while we scream."

"He does what?" Lily's voice is low.

"It's fun."

"We can be as loud as we want to be too," Jackson adds. "Uncle Mike is so funny."

I lift my hands and shrug when Lily looks my way. "Sounds like your dad has them under control."

"He calls it a controlled burn after a sugar high," Harley explains, and it makes total sense.

"This is the best Christmas ever," Jackson adds, fist-pumping the air. "I love this place."

Jackson's right. This is shaping up to be our best family Christmas ever. It's better than working all week and taking a few days off for the holidays to do what we do every Sunday. This is new and fresh, and hopefully something we'll do for many years to come, flowing through to the next generation and their kids.

Mammoth squeezes my shoulders before whispering in my ear, "You okay, princess?"

"Just wishing I could live forever," I tell him, touching his hand on my shoulder.

"Don't we all."

I'm not sure he understood exactly what I meant. I love my life, but I want to see what's next for the family and never miss a moment. I want to meet my kid's children and their children, but we can't live forever. I just hope I live as long of a life as my grandparents.

"Okay. So, dinner then drinks. It's settled." Gigi

pushes herself up from the couch and grabs Pike's arm. "We should get ready."

"I could use a shower," he says to her.

"Don't go getting knocked up too," I tell her as they walk toward the stairs.

Mammoth bends down, placing his lips next to my ear. "You want another one, princess?" he whispers, sending a wave of goose bumps across my skin.

"Nope. Not even a little bit."

He strokes my cheek with the back of his hand. "Are you sure?"

I turn my head, staring at my handsome husband. "I'm completely sure, baby. I love our life. Why? Do you?"

"I want whatever's going to make you happy."

"That's not an answer," I say softly, searching his eyes for how he really feels about the idea. We discussed this a few years ago after I miscarried, and we decided we were more than complete with two beautiful, healthy children.

"I love our life too, but if you wanted one, I'd have a hell of a time making it happen."

I press my mouth to his, loving that he'll give me whatever I want even after all these years. But he's already given me everything I wanted and more. There isn't a thing about my life, our life, that I'd change.

rocco

. . .

"BABY, you're looking more delish than anything they're going to serve at the lodge." I grab Rebel at the waist, hauling her over to me as I sit on the edge of the bed. "Maybe we should stay in."

"Oh no, Rocco Gallo. I'm not missing a good meal with the family." She wiggles, trying to break free of my grip.

I lift her shirt with my thumb, brushing my lips against her skin near her pants. "There was a time when you would've given up everything to stay in bed with me."

She lets out a little whimper as I kiss her hip bone, dragging my warm tongue on her flesh.

I pull her closer, wanting to taste her all over. "We

can be quick," I promise, moving my hand from her waist to between her legs. "One orgasm."

"Later," she says, all breathless. "We're already late."

I close my eyes and sigh. The cabin has me feeling nostalgic for the good ol' days. We're not old, but since we've had kids, things have changed. Our lives are moving too fast, and we haven't had the chance to enjoy each other in far too long. "Okay. Later."

"Daddy," Adaline calls from outside the closed door. "We're ready."

Rebel peers down at me and gives me a sorrowful smile. "It wasn't going to happen anyway, love."

"Later," I whisper, running my fingertips across her stomach before I stand. I have to adjust my cock in my jeans before I walk out the door. The last thing I want is to scar my daughters for a lifetime.

"You good?" Rebel asks, her gaze dipping to my crotch as I try to make my dick invisible.

"What do you think?" I glance down, still seeing the outline.

"Think of something horrible, and it'll go away."

Women don't understand it's not that easy to make a hard-on go away once it's there and ready to go. I can think of all the bad shit I want, but it wouldn't make it magically disappear.

And when I look at my wife, wearing a pair of tight black pants, looking beautiful as always...it does nothing to help my situation.

"Think about having another baby."

"Reb, come on. That won't help."

"Shitty diapers. Baby vomit," she adds. "What about sucking the snot out of their noses."

I grimace, remembering the worst parts of babies. "Done. I'm ready."

Rebel chuckles as she grabs a hat off the chair near the dresser. When she opens the bedroom door, Liv and Adaline are standing there all dolled up in bulky sweaters and black leggings. They're a spitting image of my wife, and I hate to think of them grown up and all the men I'm going to have to beat to keep them safe.

"Hey, babies," I say, placing my hand on Rebel's back to head to dinner. "You two look so pretty, just like your mommy."

They beam with pride, loving the praise.

"Can we make a snowman later?" Liv asks as she walks out front toward the stairs.

"Yeah, sweetheart. Whatever you want."

"Aunt Suzy said there's a blizzard coming, so the snowman may have to wait until tomorrow."

Adaline looks at us over her shoulder. "What's a blizzard?"

"Sweet Jesus," I mutter, realizing we've kept our children sheltered by not visiting more cold-weather places.

Rebel elbows me in the ribs but doesn't miss a beat. "It means we're going to get a lot of snow."

"What's a lot?" Adaline asks, wanting to know more. She always does. One answer is never enough for her.

"Feet."

Adaline's eyes go wide. "Feet?"

Rebel shows her how much with her hands. "It's going to be about this much."

"Yes!" the girls cheer as they run down the steps.

"Careful," Jo says to them before they have a chance to make it to the bottom.

She and Nick are waiting for us at the bottom of the steps, already wearing their coats and ready to head to the lodge.

"I hope the food is good," he says, rubbing his stomach through his coat. "I'm freaking starving."

"I bet they have bison," Jo tells him. "Something exotic because we're in the mountains."

"Did you see a bison around here?" he asks.

She shrugs. "Nope, but that doesn't mean it won't be on the menu."

He grabs her scarf off the counter and wraps it around her shoulders and neck. "Well, I'm hungry enough I could eat an entire bison all by myself."

"When aren't you hungry?" she replies and laughs.

A second later, Valentino and Maria come barreling down the steps.

"Don't forget us," Valentino says as soon as his feet hit the wood on the main floor.

"Everyone have everything they need? It's not a quick walk back."

"We're walking?" Adaline whines and stomps her foot. "Can't we drive?"

"We're going to enjoy nature," my wife answers, making all of us take this trek on foot. "We think it's the best way to enjoy our time."

"Who's we?" I ask, because I sure as hell didn't say I wanted to hoof it a quarter-mile in the snow and cold to the lodge.

"Me, Jo, Olive, and Opal."

"Women," Stone says as he walks into the house from the front porch. "Bundle up. It's cold as hell out there."

"Great," Carmello mutters. "I'm already over the cold, and it hasn't even been a day."

"It sure makes me appreciate the weather in

Florida a hell of a lot more," Stone replies, flexing his hands in his gloves.

I always liked the look of winter clothes, but now that I've experienced them, they're not worth it in the slightest. They're too tight, too claustrophobic, and way too hot when you're inside.

My phone buzzes in my pocket, and I fish it out.

Tamara: Where the hell are you?

Shit.

"We better go. They're waiting on us," I tell the group as I send a message back to Tamara to let her know we're on our way. "If we're any later, we're never going to hear the end of it."

"We're taking the trucks," Stone says, making an executive decision. "We're late and don't have time to hike through the snow. It'll be faster if we drive."

"Fine," Opal says with a sigh. "But we're taking a hike tomorrow."

"Thank God," Rebel whispers to me as she loops her arm around mine. "I didn't want to hike all the way to the lodge."

I bend my neck, kissing my wife on the forehead. "We can always go on our own, baby. Don't do what you don't want to do, no matter how much Opal, Olive, and Jo pressure you into anything. No one bosses my wife around but me."

She giggles and raises an eyebrow. "You sure about that?"

"Not in the slightest," I tell her, knowing she's the boss and I don't have a problem with her telling me what to do as long as it makes her happy.

luna

...

WHEN WE'D CHECKED IN, I hadn't noticed the restaurant, but now that I'm standing inside, I have no idea how I missed it. Grand doesn't even begin to describe the rustic cathedral ceiling, two-story rock-covered fireplace, and long tables filling the expansive space. It looks like something straight out of a medieval movie set and nothing like I'd expect to find in the present-day Carolinas.

"Wow," my twin sister Ro says as she comes to stand beside me. Her mouth's hanging open exactly like mine. "This place gets more and more impressive."

"Yeah," I whisper as my nephew Salvatore takes off, heading toward his cousins, who have already found a place to play off to the side of the dining room.

"Baby, you stuck?" Nevin touches his hand to my back, making my feet finally move. "What's wrong?"

"It's so pretty," I tell him as I weave through the chairs half filled by family.

"It's something," Nevin says as Ro and Dylan follow behind him.

"I'm starving," Ro says as her heels slap against the waxed hardwood. "I hope the food is as good as this room is beautiful."

"Don't worry, baby," Dylan says, "I've got something for that hunger."

Those words are followed by a slap and grunt.

"I want food," she tells him, no doubt slapping him square in the chest.

Aunt Fran's eyes land on us as we walk down a row. Her smile is immediate and big. "Well, don't you kids look good."

I bend down and kiss her cheek. "Are you talking to me or the guys?" I ask her.

Aunt Fran chuckles. "You know me too well, sweetheart."

"You're a horndog, Auntie."

Uncle Bear catches my eye as I straighten and gives me a wink. I smile at him, always having found him charming, even when I was a little girl and he looked more like a grizzly giant than anything else.

"Hey, Uncle," Ro says to Uncle Bear, passing over Aunt Fran because she is too busy snagging Nevin and Dylan as they walk by.

That's the thing about Aunt Fran. She loves men. Uncle Bear is her husband, but she's always said that her marital status doesn't stop her from admiring the opposite sex.

"Merry Christmas, sweethearts," Uncle Bear says, his eyes moving between my sister and me.

"You too," I say as I brush my hand over his shoulder and head to the other end of the table next to theirs, where my cousins are.

"Nice of you to dress up," Trace teases my brother-in-law Dylan.

Dylan gives Trace a middle finger. "They're new jeans and a Henley. You can fuck right off."

Trace chuckles. "I wasn't sure you owned anything other than those white tank tops so you can show off your ink and muscles."

Dylan blows kisses at Trace. "Jealous?"

Trace shakes his head as he rolls his eyes.

"Behave," Ana, Trace's wife, says to him as she places her hand on his arm. "It's Christmas. Don't be an asshole."

I take a seat across from Ana and smile at her. She's a sweetheart. Trace isn't bad either, but like all the men in this family, he can be a downright asshole when he wants to.

"Don't mind him. He's always a scrooge this time of year," Rocco tells us as we settle into our spots.

"What happened, buddy? Santa forget one of your gifts one year, and you've had a hard-on ever since?" Nevin asks Trace, busting his balls.

"No, jagoff."

"We'll get a few drinks into you, and you'll find your spirit again."

"I'm not a scrooge. I like Christmas just fine."

Nevin's hand finds my leg underneath the table, and his fingers tighten and still. "Well, this trip is about your grandparents, so wipe that scowl off your pretty face and find your Christmas cheer."

Trace leans back, throwing his arm across the top of Ana's chair, but his gaze moves toward where my grandparents are sitting. "They need to live forever," he says, his voice distant and sad.

"It would be nice if things worked that way, cousin," I say to Trace, feeling the same way. "But they don't. All good things eventually come to an end."

The thought of losing my grandparents leaves a knot in my stomach as my chest squeezes. They're the glue to our family, and life without them wouldn't be much of a life at all. Who would host Sunday dinners?

No one's as good of a cook as my grandmother, no matter how hard they try, especially not my mother.

"You guys need to stop with the depressing shit. Life is good now. Everyone's here and healthy. Stop waiting for the bad shit to come. Don't dwell on it, because when it comes, you'll regret all the time you wasted. Fuck. Look around. Life doesn't get much better than this."

Leave it to my brother-in-law to speak the truth and put us all in our places. He doesn't talk a lot, but when he does speak up, it's usually solid advice.

And he's right. Life is good...better than I ever thought possible.

rosie

. . .

I LEAN OVER TOWARD LUNA. "I got a secret," I whisper in her ear.

"What is it?" she asks without even looking at me, trying to play it cool as everyone around us talks too loudly for them to hear what we're saying. "Because I have one too."

I pull my body back, staring at my sister's profile. "What's yours?"

"You tell me first."

"I'm pregnant."

Her head snaps to the side as her eyes widen. "Me too."

Within an instant, we throw our arms around each other and squeal. No one else, besides our husbands, seems to notice us.

I squeeze my sister tightly, loving that we're pregnant at the same time. "How far?" I ask her.

"Three months. You?"

"Three months."

She gasps. "Oh my God. We're going to have babies together, and they'll be a weird type of twins."

I think about her words, wondering how close to the truth what she's saying is. We're twins. We have the same DNA, and we married brothers who, while not an exact match, are pretty damn close.

"Kind of. Yeah," I say.

"When are you telling Mom and Dad?"

"Tomorrow. You?"

"Us too," she says. "Figured there's no better day than Christmas."

"I dreamed of this. Us pregnant together."

She squeezes me again as we hug from our seats. "Me too, sissy. Me too."

"Guess we're sharing the news?" Dylan asks as he leans into our conversation.

"Ask your brother," I tell him, so Nevin can tell him their news.

"My brother?" Dylan's gaze flickers over our heads toward Nevin. "You too?"

Nevin smiles. "Yep."

They're weird. They can say almost no words at all

and somehow have an entire conversation. I always thought Luna and I were the best at that, but somehow, our husbands have gained the skill and surpassed our expertise.

"Fuck yeah, brother. Congrats."

"You too."

"What's up?" Trace asks, never missing much, especially as we're having a mini celebration only a few feet away. "Why's everyone so happy?"

Luna releases her grip on me and leans across the table, shrinking down like somehow it'll make it harder for the people around us to hear. "Don't tell anyone, but we're pregnant."

Ana gasps and covers her mouth immediately.

"No shit," Trace mutters as he turns his gaze toward his wife. "Us too."

"Fuck. Seriously?" I ask, shocked.

"There wasn't much else to do during the last hurricane," Trace replies.

"Us too," I say, breaking out into a fit of giggles.

"Looks like it was the most popular activity," Luna adds.

That's three new babies coming to the family before we hit a new hurricane season.

I let my eyes wander around the room. "Do you think anyone else is pregnant?"

Luna snorts as she places her hands on her stomach. "I'm guessing everyone here if we're any indication."

"The old people are a solid no."

"Could you imagine?" I say, glancing at my parents, who are busy holding hands and rubbing noses like they're a newlywed couple. "Shit. I'd die."

"I mean, they look like they still..." Dylan starts to say, but my hand flies to his mouth, covering his words.

"Don't finish that statement."

His eyes sparkle as his lips turn up in a smile behind my palm.

"I don't need to think about them doing that."

Luna smacks my shoulder. "How do you think we got here?"

I drop my hand from Dylan's mouth and take a deep breath as I try to push away that horrible visual. "I like to think that when we were conceived, that was the last time they did it."

Luna only snorts louder this time. "You're an idiot. Look at them."

"I hope we're still doing *it* at their age," Dylan says. "If I can still get wood, I'll be a happy man. You should be happy for your parents."

I cover my mouth, trying to stop myself from being sick. "Seriously? I can't have this conversation."

"You think Bear and Fran still do it?" Nevin asks, and when I turn my glare toward him, along with my sister, he raises his hands, "What? They're not your parents."

Dylan barks out a laugh at his brother's question. "Man, we're cruisin' for a bruisin' tonight."

"I know who's not doing *it* tonight," Luna says, raising her nose in the air as she turns her head away from her husband.

"Baby," Nevin says, touching her arm. "Don't be that way. Old people do it. It's part of life—or, at least, I hope it is, because if it's not, what's the point of getting old?"

"You think there's a point to any of this?" Trace asks as he reaches for his glass of wine. "We just need to enjoy every damn minute as it comes because someday we're going to be just as old as the rest of them in the room, staring down the barrel of the shotgun of time."

"Man, you should've put that on your Christmas card this year. It's very inspirational," I tell my cousin as I reach for the pitcher of water, wishing it was wine to make it through this evening. "You're filled with holiday cheer."

"He's turning into a grumpy old man before my eyes," Ana, his sweet wife, says as she rests her head against the side of his arm. "I can't imagine how he's going to be in thirty or forty years."

"He'll be a miserable prick," Dylan answers, "with his balls hitting his knees when he walks."

"Just like my dick does now, buddy," Trace shoots back.

This is going to be a long night and a much longer trip if the guys keep this up.

Luna leans forward and glances around our small area of the table. "You guys better start playing nice, or you're going to have a very, very crappy Christmas with nothing more than your hand to keep yourself happy and warm."

"Fine," Nevin grumbles. "But for the record, I haven't done anything wrong."

Luna shoots him a glare. "You're not doing anything to make things better, and you aren't innocent."

"Damn it," he mutters.

"Is she talking for you now too?" Dylan asks me.

"It's time we all be nicer to one another. Save the bullshit for later."

"Fine," Dylan whispers. "I'll be nice to Trace."

Trace snarls at Dylan, but there's no bite behind the look. No matter what, we all love one another, even when we're driving one another up a wall.

Almost all of us work together, and we hang out with one another when we're not at Inked. It's surprising how little we fight, considering the amount of time we spend together.

Ana elbows Trace. "Promise me you'll behave too."

Trace's sigh is loud enough to hear across the table and above the talking around us. "I promise."

"It'll be a Christmas miracle," I mumble, knowing the guys can't go very long without teasing one another.

carmello

. . .

"MAYBE THIS WAS A MISTAKE," I
whisper, staring out the window of the cabin and
pinching the collar of my sweater closed.

Ever since we came back from dinner, I haven't
been able to get the chill out of my bones. No matter
how many layers I put on or how long I sit in front of
the fireplace, I can never seem to get warm enough.

"You can say that again," Rocco replies from the
door, startling me.

I shiver as the cold air licks against the back of my
neck, and I turn to face my brother. "Whose dumb
idea was this?" I tick my head toward the snow-covered
mountains and snarl as more of the white shit falls
from the sky.

Rocco stalks into my room and comes to stand

next to me, taking in the haze of white. "The old people thought we needed to see snow."

"And we listened?"

He nods. "They didn't give us much of a choice."

"We should be spending Christmas in the Bahamas or the Maldives, wearing as little clothing as possible. Not the middle of nowhere on the side of a mountain in some Podunk cabin resort, trying to live the pioneer life."

His gaze swings to me. "Grandpa," Rocco grumbles, shaking his head. "He said he doesn't have many Christmases left and wanted something like he had in his childhood."

"He's so full of it. The man is never going to die, and he could've at least picked the Four Seasons or something a little more...upscale." I swipe my index finger across the pane of glass, wiping away the condensation caused by shoddy construction. "Without the fireplace, we'd freeze to death."

Rocco faces me and clamps his hand down on my shoulder. "I think it's time to revoke your man card, brother."

I glare at him, resisting the urge to pop him in the face. "This coming from a man who gets a regular pedicure."

"That's Rebel, not me."

I tilt my head, staring at my brother and knowing he's lying through his teeth. The man has always been into manscaping, getting regular manicures when he was younger to impress the ladies. "How's that?"

"She doesn't like my scratchy feet touching her under the covers. She books the appointment, I go. Simple as that."

"I'm heading to the bar. Who's coming?" Stone asks, leaning against the doorjamb with his arms crossed. "Or would you two rather stay here and keep going with this heartwarming moment?"

"There's a bar here?" I ask, ignoring his dig. "Where?"

He nods and points to the big building in the distance. "That's the main house. Lobby, bar, restaurant, spa."

Rocco whistles. "Maybe this week won't be that bad after all."

I squint, trying to catch a glimpse of sunlight, but I see nothing but gray and white. "Yeah, genius, but we have to walk through a snowstorm to get there."

"I have the truck warming up," Stone tells us as he grabs my coat off the chair next to my bed and throws it at me. "No one's freezing on my watch."

There's nothing else to be said.

"Who's going?" Rocco asks as I grab my coat and shrug it on.

"Everyone." Stone twirls his keys in his hand, looking like a rabid animal trying to break free of its cage. "Well, everyone except Asher and Olive. They want to stay *in* tonight." He uses air quotes when he says the last bit.

I slap Stone on the back and laugh. "Newlyweds."

"Were any of us that annoying?" he asks me when Rocco strolls up behind us as he puts on his jacket.

I stop dead in my tracks and stare at Rocco.

"What?" He lifts up his hands like he doesn't remember how he and Rebel barely left the house for a month after they tied the knot.

If I hadn't known better, I would've thought they'd waited for marriage, based on the way they couldn't keep their hands off each other.

"I thought you were going to die from starvation."

"I was eating well," he says with a smirk and hits me in the shoulder. "If you know what I mean."

I roll my eyes and grumble. "You're an asshole."

Stone starts walking down the hallway and calls out, "Come on, morons. Everyone's waiting for us at the bar, and you two are here arguing about bullshit that doesn't matter. I need a drink or ten before the lack of sunshine gives me seasonal depression."

Our feet come unstuck from the wooden floor, and we start to jog toward him.

"You know, it takes longer than a few days to get seasonal depression. I think you're in the clear, dummy," I say as soon we catch up with him.

He shrugs. "Doesn't matter. I can't sit in the room all night, and all the elders are already settled in for the night."

"Elders?" I snort, shaking my head at his use of verbiage. "You make them sound ancient. What about the kids?"

"Got them covered. All the parents are in charge of the grandkids, so we can have a night out without any responsibilities. We covered everything while you two were in your rooms dicking around."

"And our wives?" Rocco asks as he pulls a ski cap over his head, covering his ears.

"Tamara rounded them up already. They're at the bar waiting. Like I said, everyone is there," Stone says, growing impatient with our questions. "And as much as I like you two, I'd rather be with my wife."

"Well, get your ass in gear. We're walking," Rocco says.

"Fuck me," I grumble. "I don't know if I'll make it with the cold."

"Buck up, you big baby. Turn that coat on," my brother says, "and let's hit it."

"Shit. I totally forgot this thing turns on." I touch the front of my coat, trying to find the power button. "This may be the best thing ever invented."

"Your wife knows you're a pussy. It's ridiculous that you need a heated jacket." Rocco flicks the collar of my fancy jacket that's already starting to warm up. "I'm never going to let you live this shit down."

"Whatever. I don't care what you say as long as I'm not the one with hypothermia," I say before I stalk out of the cabin, heading into the blizzard to find my girl.

asher

...

I ALMOST SPIT out my beer as Rocco, Carmello, and Stone walk into the bar, covered in snow, with scowls on their faces like they're about ready to murder someone.

"What the hell happened to you three?" Mammoth asks before chuckling, not giving a single shit about their expressions.

Stone gives Mammoth the middle finger before shrugging off his coat with a groan. "Rocco's a dumbass."

"Well, that's a given," I say, shaking my head.

Rocco's eyes move to me and darken. "I may be cold, but I can still kick your ass."

"Merry Christmas to you too, Scrooge," I tease

him before blowing him a kiss. "I'd like to see you try, old man."

"Be nice," Olive says at my side, placing her hand on my bicep. She's always a peacekeeper, even when she doesn't need to be, because we always bust one another's balls. It's how it's always been and how it always will be.

I look at my girl and smile. "He threatened me first, baby."

She raises an eyebrow.

I immediately know I've said the wrong thing. "I'll behave, but only because I don't want to end up on the naughty list."

She smirks as her gaze drops to my mouth. "I have plans for you later, and they most definitely will put you solidly on my naughty list."

I sit up a little straighter, my mouth watering and my cock hardening at the promise of a steamy evening. "Anal?"

She closes her eyes and inhales. "No, Asher. You can give up on that dream. It's never happening."

"But it's Christmas," I whine, hoping to tap into her love of the holidays as a reason to give up her ass, which I've been dying to get a piece of since the day she walked back into my life.

"I don't remember there being anything about

anal in the Night Before Christmas stories," Olive replies.

I pout, hoping she'll take pity on me someday. "That's because it was written for children and not grown men with needs."

Olive shakes her head, done with my shit. It was worth a shot, even if I knew she'd never go for it. I'll probably be on my deathbed someday, still begging for it.

"Ignore him," Tamara says as she sits down at the table next to Mammoth. "My brother is a dumbass, and men never stop trying when it comes to our asses."

"He's not so bad," Olive tells Tamara.

Mammoth slings his arm around my sister's chair and places his hand on her shoulder, pulling her toward him. "And some women are more than happy to give up a little ass because they enjoy it too."

Tamara turns a bright shade of red. "Shut up."

My stomach lurches, and bile rises in my throat. "Dude, that's my sister."

He turns his steely gaze toward me. "And she's my wife."

"I don't want to hear what you two do behind closed doors."

"I don't want to hear you beg your woman for ass

play either, but here we are," he says with a challenging smirk.

"New topic," Olive interrupts before I have a chance to say a few more choice words to my brother-in-law. "I could use another drink."

Those words are spoken to me, and I take the hint. "I'll get the next round." I peer over at my sister and Mammoth. "Same?"

They nod, still cuddling up to each other, whispering about something I can't make out. But I'm sure they're words I don't want to hear.

Stone follows me to the bar, rubbing his hands together like he's still frozen from their walk. "I couldn't do this forever."

"What?" I ask as I lean against the bar, placing my heavy boot on the rail a few inches above the floor. "The cold?"

He nods. "And the clothes."

I peer over my shoulder at Olive, who's looking cute as hell in her sweater, but I much prefer her in tank tops. "I hear you on that one, cousin. Getting naked is a damn near ordeal with all these layers."

"Quickies are impossible."

I snort at the remark. "Could you imagine trying to bag a chick in the bathroom of a club in the middle of winter?"

"Where there's a will, there's a way, but I don't think I was built for it. I'll always live in the sunshine."

I sigh. "Me too, but I have to say, this feels like Christmas—or at least the way it's always sold on television."

"Gramps did good," he adds as the bartender strolls our way.

"Another round for the table," I say to him, hoping he remembers what everyone ordered. In a place this small, it can't be that hard.

"Got it," the older gentleman says before turning to Stone. "And you, sir?"

"Whatever you have on draft and a white wine."

"Coming right up." He wanders away, leaving us to talk while he gets the drinks ready.

Stone bumps my arm with his elbow. "Who would've thought two years ago this is where we'd be?"

"You mean in the snow?"

He rolls his eyes. "God, you're a dumbass. I mean married."

"Ah," I whisper. "I thought we'd stay single forever. I couldn't imagine a time when you wouldn't be my wingman."

"You were my wingman, Ash. Not the other way around."

I chuckle and elbow him back. "Whatever lies you need to tell yourself, buddy."

He grunts his disapproval. "None of it matters now, but I was the one to get married first. Just saying."

"Fine. I'll give you that one. Happy?"

He gives me a big, dopey smile. "Very."

The man is so easily satisfied. "Things good?" I ask him.

"Couldn't be better."

"Same," I tell him.

"Everything okay?" Olive asks, joining us at the bar.

I wrap my arm around her, pulling her to my side. "Yeah, sweetheart."

"You sure? Looked intense," she replies.

"We're old," Stone blurts out. "We've become old people."

Her eyebrows furrow as she gawks at Stone in confusion. "What?"

I kiss the top of Olive's head, burrowing my face into the sweet softness. "He's being an idiot, Oli. Ignore him."

"Well..." she mumbles like it's not surprising. It is Stone after all.

"He's worried we are becoming boring. That's what he's trying to say," I explain further.

She curls tighter against my body. "You're the furthest thing from boring." The look on her face is nothing short of sinful.

"We should go sledding," Stone adds. "We've never done that."

I sigh, knowing I'll have to do it for Stone's sake or he'll harp on our elderly status the entire trip. "If it'll make you happy, I'll go with you."

He snatches me away from Olive, pulling me into a giant bear hug. "Fuck yeah, man. You've made my year."

"Doesn't take much," I mutter as he nearly squeezes the life out of me while Olive snickers behind us.

stone

. . .

"COUNT ME OUT," my sister says, shaking her head back and forth like she's possessed. "Never happening."

"Why not?" I ask her, confused.

"I'm terrified."

"Of sledding?"

"Yep," she snaps and crosses her arms, something she does when she's dead set on something and there's absolutely no changing her mind.

I stare at her, my lips parted, eyebrows raised, and in complete shock. "How can you be terrified of sledding? Kids do it, Lil."

"Kids bounce and recover quickly. I don't."

I shake my head at her ridiculousness. "Fine.

Whatever," I mutter, knowing there's nothing I can do to make her feel different or ease her mind. "Can Jett come?"

Jett lifts his hands and does a quick headshake. "I'm staying with my wife."

"You can go," Lily tells him, snuggling into his side. "You should have fun."

He places his lips against her hair. "The only fun I want to have doesn't involve a snow-covered hill."

"I'll go," Opal says as she wraps her hand around my forearm. "I went sledding once, and it was a blast."

I peer down at her as she rests her cheek against my arm. "You're not afraid?"

"That's part of the fun." She smiles when she says those words, and she squeezes my arm. "You'll see."

"Thank goodness you're not a shit in the pants like my sister and her *man*, and I use that term loosely."

Jett's glare is immediate. "Fucker."

I smirk, loving when I can yank his chain. "I know you're getting up there in years and don't want to risk breaking a hip or some other old-person injury. We all must know our limits, and you clearly know yours."

"I'm not that much older than you, asshole."

"But you are older," I tell him, twisting the knife of truth a bit more.

A strong hand clamps down on my shoulder, and I

lean to the side, trying to alleviate the sudden pain. "Wanna say that again, asshole?" Mammoth grumbles above me.

"Nope," I grit out, unable to take a deep breath until he releases his grip on me.

"Didn't think so."

I turn my head and tip my face upward, looking at my cousin's husband. "You going for sure, then?"

He stares at me and doesn't say a word. I know without a response that he wouldn't miss something that could give him a thrill. His nickname should've been Daredevil and not Mammoth. Sure, he's a big dude, but he loves a rush, even if it could cause his life to end prematurely.

"Mom may shit a brick," Lily says, breaking the tension.

Tamara snorts. "That's one way to put it. She won't be happy, but I bet our dads go, though."

"Not if our moms have anything to say about it," Asher adds. "They kill all the fun."

"It's what we women do, don't you know that?" Olive teases Asher, giving him a little elbow to his ribs. "Our sole mission in life is to kill your happiness and ability to off yourselves at a too-young age due to stupidity."

"We'll ask them tomorrow at breakfast and go

tomorrow night after we open presents," I tell everyone. "It'll be the perfect way to spend Christmas."

"Sounds delightful," Lily mumbles.

nick

. . .

THERE'S enough paper scattered on the floor to
create a small library any reader would be proud of.
"Man, this is bananas," I say, staring at the chaos in
front of me.

"It gets worse and worse every year," my dad says as
he stands next to me, watching as the youngest
continue to rip open their presents. "But I wouldn't
have it any other way."

"I miss being that age. Everything felt so possible."

Dad places his hand on my shoulder. "Everything
is still possible, Nick. A little of the magic may have
worn off as you grew older, but that doesn't mean you
can't have everything you want."

I turn to look him in the eyes, the same eyes I have

and got from him. "I have everything I ever wanted and more, Pop."

"Then count yourself lucky, son. There're a lot of people who will never be able to say that."

"I know, Pop. I know." I turn my gaze back toward the kids as they lose their minds over toys that are way too expensive. They're more spoiled than we were at their age, and that's saying something. While we tried our best not to go overboard, our parents spent a small fortune and quite possibly cleared out more than a store or two.

"What's wrong?" Ma asks as she comes up behind us, peeking between us at the kids. "Did I miss something?"

Pop reaches back and wraps an arm around her, hauling her between us. He kisses her temple as she relaxes into him. "Just enjoying the kids."

"I love Christmas," she says and finds my hand, lacing her fingers with mine. "And this is the best one I've had since you were a little boy. Grandpa had a great idea."

"Maybe we'll make it a tradition," Pop says.

"I'd love that," she tells him. "What do you think, Nicky?"

The little boy that's buried deep inside me always creeps out when I'm near my mother—and especially when she calls me Nicky. "I don't care where we are, Ma, as long as everyone is there."

Jo moves our way, carrying a mug. "I thought you'd want this," she says as she lifts the mug in my direction.

I glance down, taking in the melting whipped cream and an overabundance of tiny marshmallows. "My new favorite."

"It doesn't hit quite the same way when it's ninety outside," she says as I take the hot chocolate from her hands.

"There are some upsides to the weather here." I give her a wink, remembering how we made love in front of the fire in our room last night.

Jo blushes as she averts her eyes from my parents, who seem oblivious to what we're talking about.

"Better be careful, or you two are going to give us another little one by next Christmas." Pop nudges me with his shoulder. "And if that happens, your mother would be ecstatic."

"And you?" I ask him.

"I always regretted not having more children, so I'm hoping you rectify that with a bunch of grandkids. Time's ticking too, kid. I'm getting long in the tooth."

"So, you'd be happy, then?" I say, trying not to get too buried in my feels about my dad's statement. He's a man of very few words, so he puts a lot of meaning into what he says.

I've often wished my parents had more than me. I was lucky enough to be surrounded by a lot of cousins, which helped fill the void, but I always yearned for a brother or sister. It's why we have two, but I'm not against adding another one.

"Over the freaking moon," he replies with a soft smile. "There's nothing better than being a grandpa."

"Being a grandma," Ma says as she wraps her arms around my father's waist. "And I'm waiting for the day I get the call that another one is on the way. You couldn't have too many kids."

"Uh," I mumble, "there is such a thing as too many kids."

"We should try for another one," Jo says like she's talking about running to the grocery store to pick up another carton of eggs.

I can't stop the smirk from spreading across my face. "Trying is my favorite part."

"That's what I want for Christmas. Another baby."

"It's the most expensive gift there is," Pop says, laughing because that shit is absolutely no lie.

It would be cheaper in the long run if I bought her

a diamond necklace with the biggest freaking rock they had in the jewelry store.

"We'll start tonight," I tell her as I bring the hot chocolate up to my lips, staring her straight in the eye.

She blushes again but doesn't say no.

"Baby, this is way too much information for us oldies." Ma shakes her head. "Some things are meant to be kept private."

"You two are the ones who said we should try for another. I'm just making it clear that I'm going to start as soon as possible. I didn't go into details."

"Men," Ma mutters under her breath because Dad and I have driven her half mad our entire lives. Our logic doesn't always match hers, even if it makes complete sense to us.

Valentino jumps up from his spot on the floor and hauls ass in our direction, carrying something out in front of him. I squint, trying to make out the blurry shape, but it's hard with his speed and the wrapping paper flying up from the floor as he kicks his way toward us. "Dad. Look." He thrusts his arms upward, showing off a super-sweet bow and arrow.

"Wow," I say, genuinely surprised by the gift. "Who gave that to you?"

"Me," Dad says. "Kid needs to learn some survival skills, and there's no time like the present."

"Isn't it amazing?" Val says, almost buzzing with excitement.

"It's something," Jo replies instead of me, but she's way less enthusiastic about the present.

"I'll teach him too. We can learn safety and how best to use it. Don't worry, Jo. He won't get hurt."

"I worry about the other kids more than my own," she tells him, knowing Val can be a wild man at times, but my dad will drill safety into his skull so he knows not to point the bow at a person.

Val throws himself at my dad, who catches him before he has a chance to bounce off the big guy. "You're the best grandpa ever."

I pull Jo against me and put my mouth next to her ear. "Don't worry, baby. He'll be safe with my father."

"I know. I'm just not ready for him to grow up." Jo curls into me and sighs. "I wish we could keep him little forever, but we can't."

I kiss her hair, hating how quickly time is passing. "I know, Jojo. All we can do is try to enjoy every minute and take none of it for granted."

She tips her head back, staring up at me like the world revolves around me and no one else is around us. "When did you get so wise?"

"The day I met you. I was a dumbass before that."

"No truer words," Pop mumbles at our side.

trace

. . .

"I'LL NEVER GET over how lucky I am to be here. My father couldn't have picked a better man to kidnap."

"Babe." I stare down at my wife; her memory of that day and the seriousness of it never ceases to amaze me. "He was going to kill me."

She places her hand on my chest and leans into my space. "But he didn't," she whispers.

"Because of you."

She giggles. "He wasn't going to."

I raise an eyebrow, waiting for her to admit the truth.

"Not personally, at least. My dad never got his own hands dirty. The moment I laid eyes on you, I knew you were the one, but I never imagined you'd come along with all this." Her gaze moves around the room that's bursting at the seams with family members. "I'm the luckiest bitch in the world."

"Hey now. Don't call my wife a bitch. She was made for me, and there isn't a thing I don't like about her."

Ana rolls her eyes. "You're such a liar."

"You better change your attitude, little girl, or you're going to get nothing but coal in your stocking."

"I can think of a sexier way for you to punish me."

I blink, processing her statement and trying like hell not to get a boner with my entire family around. "Ah. Looking for a little pleasure-and-pain combo, sweetheart?"

Her eyes twinkle with delight as she twists a little in my arms, pretending to be coy. "Maybe, but only if I deserve it."

I kiss her forehead, letting my lips linger against her skin. "Always keeping me on my toes, baby. I love you and your ability to keep things interesting."

Her body sags against me as she exhales. "Is that a no, then?"

I laugh as I pull away to see her face. "It's a definite yes."

Rocco clears his throat as he sits down at our table with Rebel. "Don't let us interrupt."

I grumble under my breath about my brother being a complete asshole. He's always had a knack for showing up at the worst times and spoiling everything.

"Be nice," Rebel tells him. "It's Christmas."

A second later, Carmello and Arlo join us.

"This may be my best Christmas ever," Arlo tells Carm, completely ignoring us.

"Baby," Carmello says as he reaches for her hand and lifts it to his lips. "Only the best for my girl."

Rocco groans, earning a smack to the chest from Rebel. "What was that for?" he asks her.

"Being a Debbie Downer." She raises a challenging eyebrow, ready to go toe-to-toe with my brother at any time. She's perfect for him. Someone besides Carmello finally calls him on his shit on a consistent basis, and it's glorious to watch.

"All my boys in one place," Ma says as she comes up behind Rocco and places her hands on the back of his chair. "And my girls too."

The women beam, always loving praise from my mother. She loves them just as much as she loves us. Maybe more. I know Mom always wanted a girl. I've heard the story a million times about how they tried two times, but it never happened. She didn't risk a third pregnancy because three boys were more than enough, and she worried she'd end up with even bigger handfuls.

"Hey, Ma," Carm says, sucking up like he's trying to please her to get the better Christmas gifts.

She reaches her hand out and runs the backs of her fingers against his cheek. "Hey, baby."

"Join us," I tell her, ticking my chin toward the open chair next to Ana. "We've barely seen you this trip."

"Your father," she says with a sigh as she slides into the empty chair. "He loves this weather. I can't keep him in one place very long."

"I love it for different reasons," Ana says with a small giggle.

Ma laughs. "It's the perfect snuggle weather, isn't it?"

I open my mouth to tell Ma snuggling is the last thing that's on our minds in the cold with a roaring fire, but Ana squeezes my hand as a warning to keep my big mouth closed.

"It is," Ana says, always keeping things PG around my ma, even though she doesn't have to because my parents are the original superfreaks.

It's one of the things I've always loved about them. They're unapologetic about every aspect of their lives. They do things on their own terms and give absolutely no shits what anyone thinks or says about them.

"Since you're all doing so much *snuggling*, I'm hoping we'll have a few additions to the family by Halloween," Ma says, gazing across the room to where my father is standing, like she's talking about the weather forecast tomorrow.

Rebel nearly spits out the drink she'd just taken a sip of.

"Sweet Jesus," Rocco mutters. "I hope not. Two is enough for me."

Ma swings her gaze back toward my brother with a smile that barely touches her cheeks. "I thought the same about you three, but looking back, knowing what I know now, I'd have ten if I could do it all over again."

I nearly choke on my own saliva. "Ma, be serious. We were enough."

Ma's smile widens this time. "You three are perfect, baby, but at the end of it all, the only thing we have is one another. You can never have too many people you love around you."

"But ten kids?" Carmello asks, his voice almost cracking at the thought of adding seven more of us. "That would've been a freaking nightmare, Ma."

"I was told having one wasn't easy, but I wouldn't know because I had to go above and beyond, having twins. But at least you two came with a built-in buddy. Inseparable from the beginning and kept each other constantly entertained."

"That's the only thing that's easy about having twins," Pop says, coming up behind Ma. He slides his hands over her shoulders and leaves them there as he bends over and kisses her cheek. "Wouldn't you say, sweetheart?"

"We somehow made it through," she whispers, "but I wouldn't want to repeat the nighttime feeding schedules of two infants."

"And so many shitty diapers," he adds as he straightens and looks over the table at us. "But every single one was worth it to be here right now, surrounded by all of you."

"Look at Pop getting all sentimental," Rocco says as he gazes up at our father. "Age is softening you, old man."

Pop's eyes narrow on my brother, looking lethal. "I can still kick some ass, kid. Doesn't matter how old I am. Don't count me out until I'm buried six feet under the dirt."

The man's glare was enough to snap us in line when we were young. He never put his hands on us and barely raised his voice, except when we were being complete assholes, which happened from time to time.

All he had to do was look in our direction, and we stopped our shit in a hurry.

"I believe it, Pop. You're the original badass."

Ma chuckles as she reaches across her body to place her hand on my father's where it's stayed on her shoulder. "It's the reason I fell in love with him."

"Your mother hated me at first," he says.

"I never hated you."

Pop rolls his eyes. "Baby, I had to handcuff you to the bed so you wouldn't run away."

She peers up at him and cocks her head. "You kidnapped me."

He leans down, bringing his face close to hers as he smirks. "I was saving your life, sweetheart, but you were hell-bent on testing the limits of your ability to keep breathing."

Ma slowly turns her head back to face us like they're discussing some mundane memory. "Well, I was trying to mix things up."

Pop tips his head back, cursing under his breath for a solid ten seconds before he looks at us again. "I have no idea how we had three boys who didn't crave danger and excitement."

As soon as those words are out of his mouth, Rebel starts to choke on her drink. She pounds on her chest, trying to laugh at the same time, because we hid so much from our parents. They never would've let us out of their sight if they'd known about half the shit we did when we were younger.

"You okay, baby?" Ma asks her.

Rebel nods and coughs. "Swallowed wrong."

I have never been so happy to have someone choke at the perfect time, thankful for changing the direction of the entire conversation.

sal

...

"ARE YOU SURE ABOUT THIS, GRANDPA?" my sweet little Gigi asks as she holds my arm like I'm breakable.

I may be older, but I'm still strong. Still healthy. Still have my mind. That's saying a lot at my age. The love of my family and a good woman have kept me going.

But my children and grandchildren see me as fragile and weaker than my former, younger self. When I look in the mirror, I see a face I don't recognize. A man who's lived a full life with lines etched in his skin to show the paths he's traveled.

Inside, I feel like a young man. I think I am one, but every time I catch a glimpse of myself, I'm momentarily dumbfounded.

And at times like this, when my grandchildren worry for my safety when I'm doing something little kids do every day, I'm reminded that I'm growing older and will never be thought of the same way as I was when I was younger.

"Sweetie," I say to her as gently as I can, "I don't plan on dying today."

She leans into my space and drops her voice. "But you could still get hurt."

I chuckle, keeping the mood light. "I could get hurt climbing out of bed too, but somehow I've done it thousands of times and I'm still kicking."

"Grandpa," she scoffs.

I know grandparents aren't supposed to have favorites, but Gigi has always had a special place in my heart. She's the oldest grandchild. My first. The moment I laid eyes on her, I was a complete and utter goner. The little girl had me wrapped around her finger and hasn't let go...even today.

"An old man still needs to live, baby," I explain, trying to alleviate her anxiety about me barreling down the side of a mountain on a piece of plastic.

"But I want you to keep on living."

I pat her hand, chuckling. "I have no plans to die today."

"I don't think anyone plans on dying. It just

happens." She's so serious when she speaks, and I can feel her panic.

"Gramps is the OG daredevil of the family," Joe says as he comes up next to us. "He'll be fine."

"See," I tell her, ticking my chin at my son. "I'll be fine. This is nothing compared to some of the things—"

Joe coughs. "I don't think we need to get into your checkered past right now."

"I want to hear about his checkered past," Gigi says, but I know the girl, and she's trying to stall, hoping I'll forget all about the sled ride.

"I'll tell you about it someday when it's not freezing outside and we're not getting hypothermia."

"Hell yeah, Gramps is up here," Rocco says as he adjusts his gloves with a sled resting between his legs. "I didn't think this day could get any better, but I was wrong."

"What?" Carm asks, stalking this way, the same look of concern on his face. "Gramps. This isn't a small hill."

"Boys," my lovely wife says, ready to wade in with the grandkids and quell their fears.

She knows some of the crazy shit I've done in my life. I've been lucky enough to have a woman at my side who doesn't try to talk me out of every harebrained idea but is willing to hold my hand and even bandage my wounds when things go wonky.

Mar wraps her arm around me, clinging to me. "Let the man live a little. He'll be fine. Your grandpa is one tough cookie."

I love that even in our old age, my girl still thinks I'm tough and strong. She still looks at me the same way she did when we were young. I'm her world, just like she is mine.

Gigi chews on her bottom lip, not looking convinced by her grandmother's words. "Okay," she whispers, understanding there's no use in fighting anymore.

"I promise I'll be careful and go slow."

Mar chuckles against me, knowing me better than anyone. Going slow and being careful have never been my strong suits, but age forced those behaviors upon me earlier than I wanted.

"You want to jump on the sled with your old man, love?" I ask Mar, wishing we could go back and do everything all over again.

I don't know what I did to get so damn lucky. I have the most amazing wife, have had the best life, and don't want for anything in the world except for more time. There will never be enough of it when it comes to my family.

"There's no way in hell I'm going down that hill on my ass," Mar says, still full of spunk, but smarter than me when it comes to her safety.

"I'll walk back down with her," Suzy says as she strides in our direction, always being helpful.

"Aw, Ma. You don't want to go for a ride?" Gigi frowns. "I thought we could race."

Suzy smiles at her daughter and touches her face with her glove-covered hands. "I would love nothing more, but that hill is too big for this old woman. Your dad's going, though. Race him."

"You're not old, Ma."

Suzy's eyes sparkle in the moonlight. "That's sweet of you to say, but my bones don't like this cold and they'll never survive that ride."

"I get it. I do. Dad will have to do."

"Wow," Joe says, feeling the sting of not being the first choice when it comes to something in his daughter's life.

It's a hard thing for a dad to come to terms with. It doesn't hurt as much with boys, but there's something about daughters that strikes right at the core of a father's heart.

I gaze around the hillside, taking in my life. One amazing wife. Five kids. Eleven grandkids. And a smattering of great-grandbabies with more hopefully on the way.

This is what life is about.

It's about the little moments.

The countless memories.

Endless love from family.

The devotion of a wonderful woman.

All the money in the world can't buy what I have. If I died today, going down that hill like a bat out of hell, there isn't a thing I would change.

But if I could have one wish, it would be for this to go on forever.

COMING UP NEXT

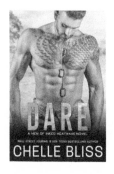

Austin Moore found his purpose in the military, but there was always something missing. He wanted what everyone in his family had... someone to call his own. But his life didn't make it easy to find a soul mate, someone to be his forever.

Sage Hill enlisted to follow in the footsteps of her father, but never wanted to be in his shadow. And when her friend ditches her at a dive bar, she catches the eye of a handsome stranger. But Sage doesn't have time for relationships, nor does she want the complication.

When Sage is stuck, Austin tries to be her saving grace and a challenge leads to a lip lock neither one of them can forget. She swore she'd never fall for a strong and bossy man like her father, but she soon learns there's more than meets the eye underneath that sexy exterior.

Part of this book was previously released as the book Fearless. Much of the content has been changed and over 100 pages of new material has been added.

Dare is also part of the Men of Inked world.

Dare releases January 30, 2024
Preorder DARE at *menofinked.com/dare*

MEN OF INKED SINNERS #1

Tate Gallo had a type – emotionally unavailable bikers who were more feral than serious relationship material.

The day she turned thirty, she decided to make a change: No more biker boys.

She deserved more. She wanted to be someone's world.

But then *he* stumbled in bloodied, bruised, and in need of help.

One look into his dark eyes, and Tate realized her life would never be the same again.

She wouldn't fall for him. She couldn't, not for her heart's sake.

But one night never hurt anyone...right?

But with one taste of his lips and touch of his hand, Tate knew she couldn't escape his pull.

Wylder was incredibly reckless, ridiculously daring,

and craved danger. He couldn't feel anything unless he was pushing the limits, chasing his own demise. But the night he met Tate Gallo, he found a new purpose —to worship the woman who made him feel something again.

But could the emotional scars of his past be easily wiped away or would they chase him, wreaking havoc on his world and the woman he came to love?

Crave releases April 2, 2024
PREORDER CRAVE HERE!
or visit *menofinked.com/crave*

Hey. Hey. Hey.

Have you read the original Men of Inked? Read where it all began...

I have a special eBook or audiobook bundle with the books in the Original Men of Inked series and you can find by *clicking here for the eBook bundle* or here for the audio bundle. You can also visit my store at *chelleblissromance.com* where there's tons of other goodies too.

As a special thank you, you'll get **10% off** the Men of Inked 9 eBook Bundle or the audiobook bundle with the discount being shown in checkout, but if it doesn't use code *inkedholiday*

A MEN OF INKED SHORT STORY

MEN OF INKED
Christmas

USA TODAY BESTSELLING AUTHOR

CHELLE BLISS

SHORT STORY

Hey Gallo Girl,

I know many of you may have never read the original Men of Inked series, but it's where this wild journey first started.

Seven years ago, I published a short story, half the size of the Inked Holiday, for readers to get a glimpse of the family at Christmas. I wanted to include it with this new short story as a little something extra in case you missed it earlier.

If you've already read it because you've been on this wild ride with me for years, you can skip it or relive the magic only the Gallos can deliver.

If you haven't read the original Men of Inked series yet, you're missing out on some of the most delicious alphas. Joe, Mike, Thomas, James, and Anthony are scrumdiliumcious in their younger years.

Happy reading and Merry Christmas!
    Chelle Bliss xoxo

mia

Twenty Five Years Ago

Stone's clapping as Pop bounces him up and down on his knee. "Stone, my boy. This is a special year." Stone laughs, drool running down his chin like a ribbon of melting snow, but Pop doesn't care. He loves Stone too much to care his pants are covered. "You don't realize it, but this has been the best year of our lives," Pop tells him, beaming with excitement. Stone claps again, his little head bobbing with each dip as Pop raises him higher and into the air.

They are adorable together. Stone loves his grandpa the most. Sometimes I think even more than he likes Michael or me. As soon as we walk in the door, he reaches for Pop to take him and won't leave his arms until we leave. It usually involves tears, as if we're taking away his favorite blanket.

"Not only were you born, but the Cubbies won the World Series too," Pop tells Stone with a smile that stretches from ear to ear.

I place my hand over my stomach, missing the feel of him moving inside me. It's hard to believe he's already nine months old. Time flew after Lily was born, but with Stone I thought it would move slower. Instead, it moved so fast it's almost like I'm watching it all take place before my eyes at double speed. It feels like yesterday that I found out I was pregnant. It was a shock to me, but even a bigger shock to Mike. After she nagged him mercilessly, he finally gave in and got a vasectomy. He was one of the unlucky one percent who went through the procedure unsuccessfully.

When he found out we were having another baby, he was excited. He claimed this proved that his manhood and virility couldn't be stopped. Naturally, he'd think it was a good thing.

"Baby, you want anything?" Mike asks, taking a seat on the armrest of the chair and wrapping his arm around my shoulder.

I glance up at him, and he's staring at Stone with the biggest smile. There's something about a man and his son. When the doctor announced that we had a boy, I thought Mike was going to beat on his chest and hold him high in the air, beaming with pride. The man prayed every day for a boy.

Don't get me wrong.

He loves his baby girl. God, Lily has him wrapped around her little finger. She always has. From the moment she was born, Mike was a goner. The little princess can do no wrong in his eyes, and she knows it. He doesn't realize it, but soon she'll be a teenager, and he's going to be in for a rude awakening.

"I'm good, love. Just watching your dad and Stone." I smile up at him, watching him as he gazes at them with the biggest grin. There's pride in his eyes every time he looks at his son.

"They love each other, huh?" Mike's thumb strokes the exposed skin on my shoulder that is peeking out from my new sweater. I still don't get why it's missing part of the sleeves, but the sales lady told me it's all the rage. I feel like I paid the same amount for a portion of the clothing.

"Yep, it's weird, almost."

"Yeah."

I place my hand on his knee and rest my head against his rock-hard chest. "Where's Lily?" I ask him, closing my eyes for a moment, listening to the steady beat of his heart

Two kids and years later and I'm still utterly and completely in love with this man. He still has the ability to make my insides quiver with anticipation when he's near.

People said we wouldn't last. A fighter and a doctor. Hell, it was probably a bet I would've taken before I really knew the man.

On the outside, he's a massive wall of muscular testosterone, but on the inside, he's nothing but a soft, loving human being. Except when he's in the ring. Then he's a beast. He transforms into someone I don't know. Someone who would pound another man's face in without even blinking. I'd never admit it, but watching him fight turns me on.

"Somewhere in the backyard with Gigi and Nick." He leans down, placing his mouth next to my ear. "We can sneak upstairs and do it in my old room." His teeth find my lobe, tugging gently. "Everyone is busy, the kids are being looked after."

I melt into him as the noise around us fades.

His lips skid across the skin of my neck before his teeth dig into my favorite spot. "Come on, Doc. I need your special medicine."

My skin breaks out in goose bumps, and I'm more than eager to steal a few moments away with my husband. Time alone has been minimal since Stone arrived. And sneaking away for a quickie sounds perfect.

"You're on, big boy," I whisper.

Mike stands and grabs my hand, pulling me up from the couch and heading toward the foyer. Pop's so engrossed in Stone that he doesn't even see us leave. Everyone else is sitting outside, watching the kids play and chitchatting while dinner is in the oven. Ma's in the kitchen, cooking and still trying to teach Suzy how not to burn food.

I giggle softly as Mike drags me up the first few steps. When I don't move fast enough for him, he hoists me over his shoulder and jogs up the grand staircase, taking two steps at a time. I bite down on my lip to stop the squeal bubbling from my throat that would be loud enough to draw attention to us.

When we're inside his room, Mike kicks the door closed and we both freeze, holding our breath because we figure our cover's blown.

"Shit, that was close," he whispers, choosing now to be quiet. Mike loosens his grip, making my body slide down his front. It's like cascading down an old-fashioned washboard.

I can feel every ripple and dip of his abdominal muscles until my feet touch the floor. Even then, my body is plastered against his, humming with excitement at his nearness. "Training has done a body good," I tell him with the biggest smile, while my hands dig into his rock-hard sides.

When I met him, I thought he was built like a brick house, but I was wrong. Over time and with more training he seems to be getting bigger and harder. There isn't an ounce of fat on the man. A year ago when he told me he wanted to get back in the ring, I was worried. After such a long absence, I wasn't sure his body could handle the grueling training and snap back.

But, damn. Mike proved me wrong.

"Whatcha thinking, Doc?" He quirks an eyebrow with a smirk. "You look like you want to eat me."

A slow, easy smile spreads across my face as I stare up into his caramel eyes. "Just thinking about how lucky I am to have you."

"Baby," he whispers before leaning forward and placing his lips against mine. He snakes his arms around my back, one hand tangling in my hair and holding me still as he kisses me deeply.

More than anything, I want to savor him, take my time making love to him, but we can't. Backing away, I say, "Michael, we don't have much..."

"Shh," he murmurs, tightening his grip on my back before he trails a line down my neck to my chest with his soft lips. He pulls my hair gently, and my body follows, giving him better access to the opening in my V-neck sweater.

I grip his biceps, digging my fingernails into the skin just underneath his T-shirt sleeve. I'm hot, but not from the overly humid December Florida air. Instead, it's from the way my husband is touching me. I shouldn't feel as needy as I do. He woke me up in the middle of the night last night, spreading my legs wide and slipping inside of me before I could fully wake. The hazy memory of it makes my skin tingle.

Reaching under my skirt, he pulls my panties down and tosses them over his shoulder before I quickly undo his pants, pushing them to his ankles. He turns us, pressing my back against the wall next to the door. His kiss deepens, growing more demanding as he presses his hot erection against me.

Lifting me by the ass, he boosts me into the air, lining our bodies up perfectly before crashing his mouth against mine. I'm breathless and needy, wanting to feel him buried inside of me and needing another orgasm like it's part of my life source. Mike runs the tip of his cock through my wetness before pushing inside, and my legs wrap around his back, taking him deeper and wanting all of him.

He starts with long, languid strokes, causing my

slow-burning desire to ignite into a wildfire of lust. The heels of my bare feet dig into his ass and try to pull him forward quicker. The leisurely pace teases me, taunting me with an orgasm that's just out of reach.

"Faster," I moan, digging my shoulder blades into the wall and bearing down on him.

Mike smirks and grips my ass cheek rougher in his palm as he increases his strokes. He's pounding into me; the photo on the wall next to my head bounces with each thrust. My toes begin to curl, and my muscles strain with the building orgasm.

Mike's grunts become deeper and his hips move faster, slamming into me so roughly that my back begins to ache from the assault against the wall. The mix of pleasure and pain, along with his massive cock inside me, sends me over the edge.

Mike covers my mouth with his when I get a little too loud and quickly follows with his own climax. Even after we both catch our breath again, we don't move. It's too quiet, too comfortable to pull apart and go back downstairs. We both have the same thought. We want to stay in this bubble of bliss for as a long as possible.

"Mike!" Joe's voice echoes through the hallways outside the door.

We both make a face at each other, knowing our moment is gone.

"I love you," I whisper to my husband, who is still buried deep inside of me.

"Love you too, Doc." He smiles and slowly lowers my feet to the floor. He starts to pull up his pants when there's a knock at the door.

"Yo, asshole. Get your cock out of her and come downstairs."

Our eyes meet, and we both break out into laughter. We weren't as sneaky or probably as quiet as we thought we were. Joe doesn't care. He and his wife, Suzy, have snuck away more times than I can count to do it all over the house. In reality, every person in this house has, at one time or another. Gotta get it when you can.

"Coming," Mike tells him as he fastens the top button on his jeans.

"Do I look okay?" I ask as I shimmy my panties up my legs and try to right myself.

"That shade of pink is amazing on you."

I give him a "What the hell are you talking about?" look and move my hands over my outfit, showing him there's not a thread of pink on me. "Pink?"

He steps forward and rests his hand against my

face, stroking my cheek with his thumb. "You have that well-fucked glow about you." He smiles.

The pink he's referring to turns into the brightest shade of red. "Damn it," I grumble.

He kisses me with tenderness, his hand still on my face, and the embarrassment that flooded me moments ago vanishes. We're not kids anymore. We weren't sneaking off to have premarital sex. The one thing I've learned about the Gallos, even his parents, is that everyone has a healthy sex life.

"We better go," I tell him when I feel the dull ache between my legs starting to return.

He nods and adjusts himself in his pants. "Going to be a long day. I may pull you into another room later."

I press my hand between his solid pecs and smile up at him. "I may just let you."

***

When we walk down the staircase, trying to act like nothing happened, Joe's waiting in the foyer with the girls. His arms are crossed in front of him with Lily and Gigi on either side of him, and from the look on his face, I'd say the girls are in trouble...again. They're staring at the floor as tears trickle down their splotchy red cheeks.

I drop to my knees as soon as I'm in front of Lily.

"What happened?" I move my eyes between Joe, Lily, and Gigi. My heart's racing because I can't imagine what has them in tears.

They've grown up so fast. Too fast for my liking. The biggest problem is they're thick as thieves and usually getting into some sort of trouble, but rarely are they in tears.

"Our lovely children thought it would be funny to convince Nick to strip down naked and run through the neighbor's yard."

I'm shocked. "What?" I gape.

Mike places a hand on my shoulder as if to steady himself. "Why in God's name would they do that?"

Joe blows out a breath and clenches his fist. "Well, I guess Nick has a crush on the neighbor girl. Our innocent little girls told him that the way to get her attention would be to run through her yard naked, singing 'Jingle Bells.'"

I have to bite the inside of my cheek not to laugh. Jingle Bells? These two little mischief-makers will be the death of Joe and Mike. They have no idea what's coming because we haven't even hit the teen years. It's going to be hell.

Mike digs his fingers into my shoulder. "What the heck were you two thinking?" His tone is biting.

"Dad," Lily says with a sniffle.

"Don't Dad me, li'l girl. Why did you tell Nick to do that?"

Joe glances down at Gigi, quirking an eyebrow, waiting for her to respond. "You have anything to say, Gigi?"

"Well..." she says, kicking at the tile floor with her eyes downcast.

"Lily, why?" Mike pipes in when Gigi pauses.

"Listen," Gigi says and looks me right in the eyes. "When my mom and dad want to show each other how much they like each other, they always get naked. We wanted to help Nick get Poppy's attention." She glances up at her father with a sad smile. "We didn't know we did anything wrong, Daddy."

"You too, Mommy," Lily says to me. "You and Daddy wrestle sometimes, and you said it was just how you show each other you love one another." And I'm horrified and a little embarrassed.

Joe's face is pale, and he looks more uncomfortable than I do. "We'll talk about this later. You and Lily go wash up for dinner. We'll see if Santa comes tonight. You two just earned a spot on the naughty list," Joe tells them.

"I told you it was wrong," Lily tells Gigi with a snarl. "I'm not going to get my tablet for Christmas because of your stupid idea." Lily rolls her eyes and starts to walk away, dragging her feet with each step.

Gigi peels away from Joe, walking next to Lily, and swings her arm over her cousin's shoulder. "Don't worry," Gigi whispers. "Santa's already in the air, and our gifts are in his sleigh. You'll get your presents."

The girls seem to forget that we can hear them. Even though they try to whisper, they're doing a shitty job of it. They've never been able to be quiet a day in their lives.

"You think?" Lily asks, glancing at Gigi.

Gigi nods. "Next year, we have to be extra good now, though."

"Darn," Lily says.

"I know. It's going to suck."

Joe, Mike, and I look at each other and bite back our laughter until the girls disappear to the back of the house, and then we lose it.

Joe sobers first and rubs the back of his neck. "We're in so much fucking trouble with them."

"Ya think?" I laugh.

Mike shakes his head, rubbing his forehead with his fingertips. "So much fucking trouble."

"Where's Nick?" I ask.

"Getting his ass chewed out by Thomas." Joe smiles. "I'd hate to be him."

Mike pulls me into his side and kisses the top of my head. "Poor kid."

"What are we going to do, Joe?"

"I think we're going to have to talk to them about nudity and sexuality."

"Fuck," Mike groans. "They're ten, for shit's sake."

"Dude, they just made Nick run around with his cock waving in the air. I think it's time for that talk," Joe laments.

"Jesus," Mike says. "This is Mia's department."

I slap his stomach to give him a reality check. "This is an us department, jerk. I'm not talking to Lily about sex by myself."

Suzy strolls into the hallway, glancing into the living room behind her. "Why do Gigi and Lily look like they've been crying?"

Joe wraps his arm around her waist when she's close enough and hauls her into his side. "You don't wanna know, sugar."

"Can't we have one day of peace?" she asks, hugging him tightly.

"I don't think I'll ever have another day of peace with three girls to raise."

We all laugh because we know his words are a sad, sobering truth.

"Wait til they date," Suzy says, looking up at her husband.

The moment Lily starts dating, I know everything is going to spiral out of control in a hot minute, and I dread the day. Mike isn't going to let a boy near his baby girl without a fight.

"I'm locked and loaded when that day comes."

"Me too," Joe tells Mike with a nod.

"You two are crazy," Suzy says with a small giggle. "Boys aren't that bad."

"Walk with me," Joe tells Suzy, placing his hand on the small of her back and ushering her out of the hallway. "Let me tell you what Nick just did."

Mike and I are trailing behind them, waiting for when she finds out exactly what our innocent angels encouraged their little cousin to do.

Joe whispers in her ear, and I know the moment he says the words because she stiffens. She stops walking and turns to face him. "What the frick? Seriously?"

"Afraid so."

"Oh, my God. We're horrible parents," she says, covering her face with her hands.

"No, we aren't," I tell Suzy, knowing exactly how she feels. "We're human. But it's time for the birds and the bees."

"This is bullshit," Mike says, being the pain in the

ass he is. "Pop never gave us that talk. I don't even know what to say to a girl."

My eyebrows draw downward as my head jerks back. "He didn't give you that talk?"

Mike and Joe both shake their heads.

"Well, what the..."

"Pop just said to use a rubber and gave us each a box of forty-eight when we turned sixteen."

My mouth falls open. "You can't say that with girls," I tell them. "So, you better figure something out because I'm not doing it alone."

"They're ten," Mike reminds me, as if I forgot that little fact, and crosses his arms in front of his chest.

"Naked," I remind him. "They think that's how you show someone you like them."

Mike winces. "Don't remind me."

"What's going on?" Izzy asks as she rounds the corner and almost barrels straight into Suzy.

"The girls got in trouble," Suzy says but leaves out all the gory details.

"Thank God I have boys." She smiles proudly, finally not complaining about having a baby girl to love.

"Hey, Izzy. Did Mom or Dad give you the birds and the bees talk?" Joe asks.

I'm sure she got a different treatment than her

brothers. There has always been a double standard when it comes to parenting children.

"Mom did. I think I was like twelve."

"What did she say?"

"I didn't even know half the shit she was talking about. Basically, she told me to wait until I was married to let anyone touch me down there. She told me that it was the most sacred gift you could give anyone."

Mike almost chokes. "She did?"

"No, ya dumb fuck. She told me to wait until I got married because men are assholes and will say anything to get in my pants. She gave me a box of rubbers and brought me to the gynecologist and put me on the pill too. She figured it didn't matter anyway. With four brothers, I'm sure she assumed I'd never get laid, so why worry."

That isn't an option for Lily and Gigi.

We aren't ready for that yet. Lord, I don't know if I will ever be ready for that.

"Izzy!" James's voice carries through the house like a roar. "I need you."

"Goddamn it. I swear, Trace thinks everything should go in his mouth. I bet he's eating the Christmas ornaments again. He should be over this phase at his age."

"Oh, gawd," I groan and dread the day when Stone

starts to eat everything in sight, including Legos and other objects that aren't meant for consumption.

"Fuckin' James takes pictures of it for his Instagram. Asshole thinks Trace is the funniest little thing ever. I'm going to junk punch him soon."

"Bullshit," Mike coughs out. "I'd like to see you try. Bet your ass gets whipped."

Izzy winks, smiling at her brother. "Only if I'm lucky."

Mike's face scrunches at her words. "Yuck."

"Oh, stop the bullshit. You know you love to spank my ass," I tell him with a small giggle, but my cheeks heat at the thought of him buried inside me and his hand coming down on my ass repeatedly.

He places his hand on my ass cheek and gives it a firm squeeze. "Fuck, I love making that ass pink, baby. When I do, your pussy grips…"

"Hey," Joe says, motioning around the room. "There are children around here, man."

"Right," Mike says and bites his lip. "Have kids, they said." He rolls his eyes and groans. "They'd be fun, they said." His lip curls and he growls. "All fucking lies."

Suzy interrupts Mike's pity party. "You guys should really stop swearing so much around the children."

"I'm sorry. You're right. I'll make an announcement before dinner."

"This should be interesting," I mutter because swearing has become almost a second and more expressive language since I've become a member of this family.

"It's best for everyone if we find big-people words to use instead of the dirty ones."

"Yes, Mrs. Gallo," Mike teases her in a whiny, little kid voice because she just pulled out the teacher tone.

"You better behave, Michael, or I'm going to have Mia give you detention."

Mike stares down at me with a cocky smirk. "Only if there's oral involved."

"Boys only think about one thing," I say, shaking my head. But to be honest, when Mike's around, it's always on my mind too.

He beams with pride. "Yep."

Ma walks in with the biggest tray of appetizers I've ever seen. "They're almost here," she says with excitement. "I never thought I'd see the day when Franny got remarried."

Two weeks ago, Fran and Bear tied the knot.

"They've been gone forever," Mom says as she sets the tray down on the coffee table near Pop, who's still holding Stone and watching the video replay of the

Cubs winning the World Series for the hundredth time.

"Ma, it's been ten days since they left for their honeymoon. Calm down," Anthony tells her, coming out of the kitchen with another tray of food.

His words earn him a glare from Ma. "Hush your mouth. My best friend has been without any type of cell reception or internet for ten days. Do you know how that killed me?"

"Killed me too," Pop says sarcastically over his shoulder.

Ma gives him a death glare. "Shut up, Sal." She pushes us out of the way when there's a knock at the door, making a beeline for the foyer.

Mike and I settle onto the floor of the living room just as Fran and Maria start squealing with delight in the foyer. Joe and Suzy walk away, heading toward the front door, while the rest of us stay put. Pop's still holding Stone, Izzy and James are off with Trace somewhere, Max and Anthony are curled up on the sofa, and Thomas and Angel are standing in the backyard, watching Nick "the Streaker" like a hawk.

The kids are running around the house, their screams of happiness while playing carrying through the sprawling two-story house. The cacophony only dims when they run out the open sliding doors lining the back of the house, but they quickly return and do it all over again. They're making a circle pattern—up the staircase, around the top floor, back down, out, and back again. I'm exhausted just watching them and more than a little jealous of their endless energy.

Mike's hand is resting against my middle, stroking my stomach slowly. "Maybe I knocked you up again, Doc," he whispers in my ear, and I can feel his smile against my skin. Diapers and sleepless nights weren't my favorite, but they definitely weren't Mike's thing.

"If there's a baby inside me, Michael, I'll never have sex with you again," I whisper back, but we both know it's a lie.

"There's the big guy," Anthony says when Bear and Fran walk into the room with Ma close behind. "What the hell do I call you now? Uncle Bear?" Anthony scratches his head in confusion.

"You're an idiot," Thomas tells Anthony and shakes his head in disgust.

Pop climbs to his feet, placing Stone on his hip, and wraps his sister in a half hug. "Franny, you look relaxed."

Fran steps back, laughing nervously as she slides back under Bear's arm. "I spent ten days in bed with this big lug. I should be in a coma."

Stone yanks on Pop's beard and giggles, distracting

him from Fran's statement. "You little stinker." Pop lifts him in the air, exposing his stomach, and gives him a sloppy raspberry against his belly button.

"Why don't the girls go into the kitchen and work on dinner, and the boys can stay out here and watch the kids," Ma says, hooking her arm with Fran's and trying to pry her from Bear's body.

"Sure," I say, climbing to my feet after kissing Michael. I've been in the family long enough to know "work on dinner" is code for drink and gossip.

"We'll hold down the fort out here," Joe tells Suzy when she stands as I pass by her and pull her with me, needing a glass of wine and a little girl talk.

By the time Suzy and I step foot in the kitchen, Fran already has seven wineglasses on the island and Ma has started to pour the wine.

"Sit," Ma says, motioning toward the stools with her chin. "Fran, we want to hear all about it."

"I'm going to need more wine if we're going to talk about old-people sex."

"Stop being a brat, Izzy. You're not too far off from being old," Ma teases.

Izzy gasps with wide eyes. "I'm in my thirties, Ma. I'm far from a senior citizen."

"You're no spring chicken anymore, sweetheart," Fran says, grabbing a glass from the countertop and lifting it near her mouth. "Just yesterday, I was in my thirties. Goes by in the blink of an eye. You'll all be old soon enough."

Each of us grabs a glass, silence falling over the room as we all take a larger than usual sip, contemplating Fran's words.

Every year, time moves faster, and nothing I do makes it slow.

"So, how was the honeymoon?" Suzy asks first as the rest of us continue to drink.

Fran rests her elbows on the counter, leaning forward and holding her wineglass in one hand. "I've never experienced anything like it."

Izzy sighs loudly before guzzling the wine, holding it with both hands.

"Bear is an animal in the sack. I can't believe I can even walk after it all." She snorts against the back of her hand. "The man should've been an acrobat."

"Sounds like you had a great time," I say, feeling slightly awkward hearing about their sex life. She's not my mother or aunt, but I've grown to think of her as a friend and I love her.

"Girl, there's something about a big, muscular guy twirling you around and bending you like you're a Twizzler."

"You mean a pretzel," Max corrects her, finally entering the conversation.

"Whatever. Who knew I was so damn flexible?"

"Anthony does this thing with his..."

Izzy grunts. "Not enough wine in the world for this conversation." She grabs one of the bottles off the counter and heads back toward the living room. "I'm going to sit with the guys and watch the World Series for the millionth time. At least that won't make my stomach turn."

When Izzy storms out of the room, we giggle loudly.

"She's such an uptight princess sometimes," Max says, rolling her eyes. "We have to hear about her chains and whips all the time, but Lord forbid we talk about one of her brother's cocks."

"I don't like hearing about Sal and Maria. It took me years not to want to throw up every time Maria would talk about their sex life," Fran admits.

"Well, shit. Who else was I going to tell? You're my best friend." Maria fills our wineglasses before refilling her own. "Fran, later you can tell me all the steamy details. We don't want to make the young ones in the room faint."

"Thank you, baby Jesus," Max mutters into her glass.

"It's time." Ma pushes a stack of plates in front of Suzy and me, and we know the routine. It's the same every week and is like a well-choreographed machine. Half of us set the table and get the troops set, while the other half prep the food and carry it out.

Someday, the men will do something more than watch sports and bullshit.

mike

I get Lily situated at the children's table before coming to sit next to Mia and Stone at the adults' table. "Did you get her something to drink?" Mia asks just as my ass touches the chair.

I climb to my feet again even though I'm so hungry I feel like I could pass out at any second. "No," I grumble. "She's ten. Her legs aren't broken."

I know I'm a whiny bitch. I love my kids and wife, but there's a limit to my selflessness and it seems to be when I'm hungry. Keeping my body in tip-top shape isn't easy.

"Just do it," Mia orders me with a piercing stare while she cuts Stone's food into the smallest pieces possible. By the way she's stabbing at the meat, I'd say I pissed her off.

After pouring Lily a glass of milk, I collapse into the chair next to my lovely wife and begin to fill my plate without talking. Everyone is chattering around me, but I'm too hungry to do more than grunt.

"Should you be eating all those carbs?" Izzy asks, pointing at my plate with her fork.

"It's Christmas. This is my cheat day." I narrow my gaze at my nosy sister. "Mind your own business."

"When's the next fight?" James asks as he hands me the giant pan of lasagna.

"In a month," I tell him, scooping out the biggest helping I can get away with without getting yelled at by Ma.

"We'll all be there, son," Pop says, which makes me smile.

My big and sometimes annoying family has been nothing short of amazing. They've always supported my choice to fight, and even after I quit and decided to go back, they followed my every move. Even Mia. I thought she was going to have a coronary when I told her I missed it, but the woman told me to follow my dream, even if it included pounding someone's face in. I remember when we first met, she hated the idea of me being a fighter. She said it went against her oath or some bullshit as a doctor to watch me beat the piss out of another man. But I saw the fire in her eyes the first time she saw me fight. It turned her on, and she couldn't deny it. Even to this day, she protests violence, but I always get pussy after a match.

Max wipes Asher's face. I've never seen a baby eat as much as that little man does. When he gets older, he just may give me a run for my money.

"Let me do that, baby. Just eat," Anthony tells her, taking the napkin from her hand.

His unusual selflessness and tenderness earn him funny looks from the entire table. Anthony isn't known for his soft side, but he's changed over the years. Between Max and his kids, he's turned into a smartass teddy bear instead of the reckless manwhore he used to be.

If I'm being completely honest, all of us have changed. I'm still an asshole, but Mia makes me want to be a better person. I'm still a work in progress, but I'm getting there.

"Fine spread you have here, Mar." Bear jams a chunk of meatball into his mouth and moans. His lack of table manners sometimes makes me look like a gentleman. I think it's why I like him so much.

"Thanks, Bear." Ma smiles. "Shit. We didn't say a prayer and our thanks. Sal, sweetheart, can you start?"

There's a collective groan before forks clank against everyone's plates. I bow my head and hope the kids get so out of control that we eventually skip finishing and go back to eating.

"Behave," Mia says and puts her hand on my knee.

"Higher," I whisper with a smirk.

"I'll go first," Fran says, standing up and looking around the table. "I'm thankful for my family and my new husband. I never thought life could be this good."

"Babe, I love the hell out of you," Bear tells her and then stands. "I'm thankful for my wife and friends around this table and those who couldn't be with us tonight. And thanks to Maria for the amazing food that's getting cold."

I knew I liked this guy. My stomach rumbles, and in order to speed shit along, I stand next before Bear can put his ass in the chair. "I'm thankful for my family and my little surprise, Stone." I glance over at my little man as he shoves lasagna in his mouth with both hands.

The kids are eating at the next table, but no one seems to care. Back in the day, Ma would've knocked us into next week for not listening and saying thanks, but not the grandkids—they always get a pass.

I tune out after Mia says her thanks and stare at my plate. It's like the food is taunting me, the aroma wafting up from the dish, making my mouth salivate.

Pop stands, clinking his fork against his wineglass,

even catching the attention of the kids. "Let's bow our heads for a prayer."

Everyone grows quiet, even the kiddos, and we bow our heads and wait. Pop clears his throat before he speaks. "Today, as we're gathered here together, I want to thank God for the amazing lives we have and that everyone is happy and healthy. Not only am I blessed with such love, but..."

He pauses and gets choked up. I roll my eyes because I know where he's going before he even says the words. There's only one thing Pop loves as much as his family. The Cubs. I'd never seen him as happy as he was the day they won. His life had been made.

"But my Cubbies winning the World Series was the best day of my life. I can die a happy man."

"For the love of God," Ma mutters. "I wish everyone a happy and healthy New Year. May we continue to be blessed in the coming year. Amen."

Joining everyone else, I say, "Amen." And I quickly do the sign of the cross before grabbing my fork and digging back into my food.

After twenty minutes of gorging ourselves on an obscene amount of food, the women clear the table and kick our asses happily back to the living room, putting us in charge of the kids. We spread out around the room, leaving enough space for our other halves when they return.

I settle into the couch with Stone in my arms. He's in that familiar food coma too. His eyes are heavy and his blinks long and drawn-out. He's fighting it, unlike me. I prop him on my shoulder and rub his back, making tiny circles until he's fast asleep

I doze off somewhere in the middle of the conversation about the Cubs. The topic has become boring to me, although Pop is still as excited as the night it happened.

"Daddy." Lily yanks on my pant leg.

"Yeah?" I don't open my eyes.

"Can I snuggle with you, or are you still mad at me?"

I glance down at her and smile. She's chewing on her index finger and staring at me while she turns her body from side to side. I pat the cushion next to me, careful not to wake Stone. "Come here, sweetheart. I always want your snuggles. I love you."

A giant smile spreads across her face. She looks so much like her mother that she takes my breath away sometimes. She climbs on the couch, settling in the crook of my arm and resting her tiny hand on my stomach. "Do you have a baby in there?" she asks into the fabric of my shirt.

"No, Lily. No baby. It's only food. Only girls can have babies. Remember Mommy and I told you that when she was pregnant with Stone."

"That's not fair. I don't want to ever have a baby. Men should be able to have them too."

Joe chuckles next to me after hearing Lily's statement, and I pull her closer to my side.

"Just stay away from gross boys, and you won't have to worry about getting pregnant."

She sticks out her tongue and makes a gagging noise. "Boys are gross, Daddy."

"That's my girl." I pray she'll always feel this way.

"I'll never love a boy the way I love you," she says, melting my heart into a pile of goo.

I lock this memory away because I know soon she'll be dating and will forget the words she just spoke. Someday, I'll have to have a man-to-man with her new beau, and it isn't going to be pretty. Soon, probably sooner than I want, I'll be threatening the life of some asswad horny teenager about putting his filthy hands on my daughter, and Lily will hate me for it.

If she's ever going to get married, it'll take a hell of a man to survive my hazing. I don't know of many fools who will willingly subject themselves to me for a piece of ass. The way I figure it, if he sticks around after dealing with me, then he'd have to be doing it for love.

When the ladies return, gift opening starts. Only the kids get gifts anymore. The main event, as I call it, takes hours. There are so many gifts in the room we'd need twenty Christmas trees to set them under. It's obscenely beautiful. The kids are glowing as they take turns opening their presents.

"We have a great life," Mia says, curling into the spot where my little girl had been an hour earlier.

"I wish we could freeze time, Doc. I don't want them to ever grow up."

"I know." She kisses my cheek, nuzzling into my neck with her face. "I love you, Michael."

"Love you too, Mia." I pull her closer, careful not to smash Stone. Somehow, he's sleeping through all the noise and shrieks as each present is opened.

"We gotta wake him up." She strokes his cheek. "Stone, baby, wake up, sweetheart," she whispers. "He'll keep us up all night, otherwise."

"We're going to be up all night setting up Lily's presents anyway. Might be nice to have him with us."

"I thought we could make love by the fire." She smiles up at me and bites her lip.

She doesn't have to say another word. I pull Stone from my shoulder and cradle him in my arms. "Stone,"

I whisper repeatedly until his tiny eyes flutter open. He smiles up at me in a sleepy haze before Mia takes him from my arms.

I glance around the room, taking in the moment. My parents are on the floor with the kids, happier than I've seen them in years. Ma's beaming with pride, and Pop's already trying to make sense of the chaos of wrapping paper, boxes, and presents.

Joe and Suzy are snuggled on the floor beside the tree with Rosie, Gigi, and Luna. I don't envy the man. There's so much estrogen in that house, I'm surprised he hasn't gone mad.

Max and Anthony are whispering to each other with Asher and Tamara in front of them, ripping open their presents and throwing the wrapping paper backward onto them, but they don't seem to care.

Thomas and Angel are next to us on the couch. She's sitting in his lap with her legs hanging over the side closest to us. Nick's by Pop, showing him the new baseball glove as they talk about how someday he'll play for the Cubs.

Izzy's leaning against James as she sits between his legs with the kids near her feet. Trace, Mello, and Rocco are like three hellions, throwing things and tossing presents to their cousins like wild animals.

When I look to Fran and Bear, they're oblivious to

the chaos in the room. They're into each other. It's nice to see them both finally happy. I never would've imagined that they would be a perfect match, but they are. He balances her nutty with his crazy, and somehow, they work perfectly.

Even my cousin Morgan showed up with his beautiful wife Race. They were late, which is normal for them. Their excuse this time is Race's ovulation schedule. Instead of being here with us, they've been at home fucking like animals, trying to get pregnant. It's a reason I can get behind.

I take it all in and try to memorize this moment. The room is filled with so much love and happiness, it's almost too much to comprehend.

I wish I could hit pause and keep us here, in this moment, forever.

How I've become this lucky is beyond me. I know the moment is fleeting. Time moves on. We're getting older. The kids are growing up and will soon take our place.

Made in the USA
Coppell, TX
01 February 2024

28471530R00090